MW01134833

Equilibrium

a collection of poems

by Monica Gayle

Monica Gayle

December, 2010

ISBN: 1453822313
ISBN-13: 9781453822319

Introduction

This collection was born out of its own need for expression and the poems were written over a period of years. As the poems become public, it is my hope that something that I have written will touch a chord in you.

It is entitled **Equilibrium** because I believe that even as we accept life's swings and pulls with equanimity we share a universal longing to be centered and to find balance.

Dedication

I dedicate this collection of poems to my daughters Sacha and Karyn.
You have my love and admiration. You never cease to inspire me.

Acknowledgement

I give God thanks for His blessings. I acknowledge with gratitude the enduring love and support of my family and friends. I sincerely thank all who helped in this process.

Biography

Monica Gayle is a former foreign language teacher with an undergraduate degree in English and French and a Master's degree in Education. Jamaican by birth, she currently resides in the United States. Among her diverse interests are her love of reading, writing and travel.

Table of Contents

Equilibrium

Turbulent uneven thoughts
Chase each other through
Uneasy possibilities
Then like a cleansing in-drawn breath
Nature's balance restores to an even keel
That life, chockfull of idiocy, laughter,
Uncertainty, strength, hope and knowing.
Inevitably nature's balance
Levels out the rolls of egotistical posturing
And places the see-saw of emotions and esteem
At eye level
For it is certain that the i that so defines us
Is in life's grander sphere
Merely a line and a dot

Kindling

Where has your fire gone?
To self-defeating disdain?
Anger that flames destructive
Subsides in ashes dull, dead and gray.
Rescue the soul from its dying embers
Rekindle and energize
The nearly expired sparks of
Half-formed thoughts and
Almost dreams and
Barely wishes.
Flashes of light
Dissipate the gloom
Of useless anger
Make useful the passion.

Truths

Truths whisper in the wind
Unheard.
Ears blunted by noisy platitudes
Discern not
Truths that are simple, unvarnished, real.
Propaganda's masquerade takes center stage
Impostor
Peddling half-truths as absolutes
The volume of such deception
Masks what we could know
If we would but
Listen to the whispers
Of our soul's conscience

Duplicity

Beware the two-edged tongue
Sword-like, its double threat is inescapable
Its duality, inevitable
Fueled by deception and dissembling
Twin evils of dubious value
The careless rapier duels
Distorting meaning
Making less that which was full
The twin-edged cleaver
Handled with nervous care
Racked by endless tension
Slips and slices
Leaving none unscathed
Not deceiver, not deceived.
Sometimes challenger, sometimes defender
Playing double, double playing
With no clear win, no singular outlook.
Plagued by omissions and remissions
Duplicitous
It creates a great divide
Deep chasms where ambiguities reside.

Retreat

Like a boat resting in calm water
You sit and rock
The picture of tranquility
In a placid sea
You hold sway
Attractive, enviable
Your trim sails, your painted hull
Pattern your ship-shape world.
At peace are you
Content
Shifting gently with wind and wave
Your boat gently rocking
But not venturing into less restful seas
Loath to disturb the even keel
Of existence
Bland and rhythmic
Fearful or careful?
What if some tide turning were to
Tilt at your sails
Do you ponder ever
Would you joust or feint, thrust or parry?
Not fear holds you so loosely anchored
Reluctance rather
To revisit those churning, heaving seas
You have been there
And now choose to sit here
Amidst the gentle lap lapping of wave
And the soothing shift of wind

Anticipation

Anticipation is joy tip-toeing around
Breath held in, it is
Hope's anguish taking hold
But loosely
All aflutter, scarcely tangible
Yet keenly felt.
Excitement, anticipation's shadow
Vacillates
Between fulfillment and disappointment
Anxiety is
A thousand impatient heartbeats
Railing at the killing slowness
Awaiting
Waiting's end.

Voices and Moods

In active voice, indicative mood
I stride, I strive, I agitate.
In passive voice, subjunctive mood
I doubt, I wish, I hesitate
Deeds I relegate
Actions I delegate
Moods my voices dictate.
In acid voice, pejorative mood
I berate, I denigrate, I excoriate
A spate of negativity
Born of voice and mood
Propagates its destructive seed
In mute I bleed
I deteriorate with the need
To give life and sound
To thoughts powerful
Only because they demand a voice.
In creative voice, exultant mood
I choose to plant, to nurture, to grow
To appreciate
To balance the voices and
Banish the moods
That suffocate.

Laughter's Magic

The laughter of a child
Is the sparkle on a dew-tipped rose
It transforms.
Unfettered, unforced, spontaneous
It engages the heart
So precious, so perfect
A ripple of sunshine
Dispersing grayness
Enlivening sameness,
Be it as fleeting
As a butterfly's kiss
Laughter's melodious memory lingers
Pure joy's echo
Unaffected, free
Strikes its chord
Exerts its influence
Our automatic response
It is magical
A blessing
A respite from tears we must shed
When we hear instead
From the world of children in pain
Separated, lost, enslaved
Misery rains on these
Hostages of war, hunger, neglect
Dull-eyed, solemn-faced
Laughter eludes them.
So laugh again, child
Laugh again

Singing in a Minor Key

Singing in a minor key
Could be sounding major notes
Letting go of plaintive songs
Playing sharp notes, not flat tunes
Adding vibrant chords, some discord
Descants and mixed chants
Strong song
Singing a strong song, not a swan song
Syncopation, innovation, demonstration of
Forceful rhythm
Staccato impatient, crescendo awakening
Ripping through your overture
Making room for more
Than soft notes and lazy arpeggios
Scaling the octave, tempering the bass
Infusing skill, energy and will
Pitching your own song
Strong song, done in special key
Manifestation of obligation to humanity

Un-Knowing

Calamities unfold, untold
Unprepared we lie at night
Hoping to undream
Messes not inconsequential
That interrupt our lives
Unsought, unwelcome
Created by other hands, underhand
Topsy-turvy world from axis spinning
Out of control, tilting world
Constructing angles of discomfort
Until untilt
Unaccustomed to our new reality
Our undoing unable to undo
Unless unbowed we strive
What choice?

Seasons of the Mind

In winter's mindset mold
I'm old, too set
To move
I need the inspiration of spring
In step
To conquer the doldrums that hem in
To the seasons of the mind
I must thus take a leaf unpredictable
From nature's volume of variables
And halt the fall
The easy slip and slide
Into time-stealing lethargy
Must pump into winter's mildew
Summer's potency
Encapsulate spring's teeming energy
To rejuvenate the mind

Time Stealers

Why do we let them
So take charge of us
Our quasi bosses
Our trivial distractions
That they with time-stealing
Staleness drag us into
Days interminable
So littered with minutiae expendable
They frustrate with their tedium
These architects of eclipsed opportunity
Deceptive in their frenetic futility
Obscure and confuse
Busyness non-essential
With business consequential
Squanderers of time
They stall our momentum
Would make spendthrifts of us
As they devalue the time we value
Why do we let them?

Remembrance

Flash of white, Flash of white
His hair, his smile
You saw them both when he was there
Fleeting impression? Indelible mark?
He made them both.
If you made a connection
It was genuine and true
If you made a friend
Then you knew

Inevitability

Inevitability
I look in your direction
As a train looks towards its terminus
Waiting to trundle or rush headlong
I choose the slow ride
No rush to stare you in the face
As our loved one slides by inches
As inevitability equals mortality.
Wheels spin in my head
I ponder ways to delay you
Derail you, cause you to veer
Off track, temporarily
Pull on your brakes, but
To you time is immaterial
I sense neither eagerness nor dalliance
As you wend your inexorable way
Forward to realize your end
As you arrive at your destination
Inevitably winning
You place me reluctant and frozen
At a station not chosen
I look in both directions to see
If as it is for the train
The end of the line is also a beginning.

Change

Change understood
Change misunderstood
Changed where we stood
Different for good
Different would
Be better
If we could
Get beyond
The reality of pain
That brought us
To the place of change
Change in leaves
Change in life
Left to fend
Must bend some
Yet not break.

Tapestry

When to satisfy our yearning
Pictures unfiltered flow
From memory's lenses to
Flood the mind
Storm the heart
Visions of life
Lived and spent
Pictures so many
So fast, reeling by
Overloading the senses
Then must we shut-down
Click off, clear space and
In the shutter-slowing
Light-softening stillness
Learn to sort and weigh
The images into textures
Absorb remembered colors and scents
See anew the light, the dark
Connect the images of
Memory's legacy
To weave a lasting tapestry
From the uneven fabric of life.

Inadequacy

While we lament our inadequacies
To adequacy we lend scant value
Being merely adequate is limit and loss
Adequate mother, brother, sister
Adequate lawyer, teacher, preacher
Dismissively we chide them
Seek to challenge not laud them
As we bemoan our lack
We may feed or starve our failings
Topping up or filling in
Spaces opened by our needs
Decreasing or abating
Noises created by our fears
As we proceed, rejecting or accepting
We make our choice
To view the constraints which inhibit us
As the defining hallmark we will cling to
Or the discomfiting bulwark we must trample.

Impact

Do not mistake this action for petulance
That I toss merits and faults alike
To float away disembodied, unchecked
Blame it on a fatigued tolerance and
Patience made pointless by abuse
See that I am impelled to step clear
Of the pile of squandered excuses
That has landed at my feet
For reason insists that I not
Remain hobbled and complicit
Stuck on a path
That keeps rewinding on itself

Clarity

Would I always opt for the clarity
To say immediately what it is
That is felt and seen
Without also defining by what is not?
What risks to this immediacy?
What limitations imposed?
What layers lost?
Would not the mind, more patiently
Awakened to discovery
Find meaning
With a resonance more clear and
Full-bodied than
Its skeletally blunt counterpart
Defined in haste?

Moments

Amidst the leafy tree-tops
That create their own
Fretwork of shifting shapes
A patch of sky peeks out
To catch your attention
To hold you intensely conscious
Was it not always there
Visible through the partially curtained window?
Innumerable times your gaze has been drawn there
Yet unremarked, until this day
A beautiful moment which speaks to the heart
What else might you have missed?
You should become a collector
A collector of moments
Of messages telegraphed by eyes
Of suppressed grins and unbridled laughter
Of unexpected pleasures and rueful surprises
Of hugs and hearts and tree-top cradled skies
Of moments that peek out and
Distract from the weeds and stones
In life's path

Interaction

Disagree with me
With civility
Oppose me
Without shredding my dignity
Or run the risk
Of having your point of view
Discounted as the bleating
Of churlishness and spite
Agree with me
In sincerity
Engage with me
In harmonious rather than discordant vein
And we will have exemplified
Tolerance and mutual respect
Realize with me
In humility
That we will thus have shared
Our better selves
In authenticity and truth

Decision

Prodded to contemplate
Prospects unsought yet intriguing
Do you choose to have
The heart defer to the head
Let ideas preempt experience
Set the mind to wander
Embracing the appealing and distancing the dubious
Assessing attitudes and pinpointing pitfalls?
Relying strongly on a language of absolutes
Will you let it crystallize its hypothesis
Based on assumption and presumption
Discounting surprise or compromise?
Should you choose to reject such clinical abstraction
Allowing action to predict experience
And risk what your heart suggests
Knowing that imperfection is not necessarily failure
Then to the extent that you are able
With your hope and your will
You may shape a worthwhile journey

Giving

Mature sophisticates
We have all but abandoned
The innocent facility of our early years
To admit our need
Simply, like a child with uplifted arms
Signaling "Pick me up"
Committed nurturers expending,
Extending a heart full of empathy,
A gift
We should be careful not to make of it a burden
When wearied, we must replenish ourselves
Lest we become depleted we must
Heed the voice behind the steepled fingers
Pleading "Fill me up"
Follow the teacher with healing hands
Advising "Drink as you pour"
Prescribe for ourselves
The same good that we dispense
So readily
This is not selfishness, merely good sense

Breathing in Heart's Space

In, out
Indrawn, released
With yoga's calm
We inhale and exhale
Being with the breath
Until we find our own space
Feeling, being
The connected, the continuum
To time and space greater than our own
Poised, balanced, prone or at ease
Always the breath is our being
Grounded, planted, rooted
We breathe
Stretching, reaching, capturing
Keeping what we need, shedding the rest
Unwrapped and centered
Receiving, giving
In harmony with the breath
In, out
Indrawn, released